SCOOBY-DOO!

RAGING RIVER ADVENTURE

by Sonia Sander
Illustrated by Alcadia SNC

WB

ABDO
Spotlight

ABDOPUBLISHING.COM

Reinforced library bound edition published in 2016 by Spotlight, a division of ABDO
PO Box 398166, Minneapolis, Minnesota 55439. Spotlight produces high-quality
reinforced library bound editions for schools and libraries. Published by agreement
with Warner Bros. Entertainment Inc.

Printed in the United States of America, North Mankato, Minnesota.
092015
012016

THIS BOOK CONTAINS
RECYCLED MATERIALS

CATALOGING-IN-PUBLICATION DATA

Sander, Sonia.
 Scooby-Doo in raging river adventure / Sonia Sander.
  p. cm. (Scooby-Doo leveled readers)
Summary: A phantom eagle is haunting the gang during their vacation of river rafting. Can
Mystery, Inc. solve the mystery with time to spare?
1. Scooby-Doo (Fictitious character)--Juvenile fiction. 2. Dogs--Juvenile fiction. 3. Mystery and
detective stories--Juvenile fiction. 4. Adventure and adventures--Juvenile fiction.
[Fic]--dc23
            2015156081

978-1-61479-420-2   (Reinforced Library Bound Edition)

Spotlight
A Division of ABDO
abdopublishing.com

Daphne's cousin, Dash Blake, invited the gang to come river rafting.

He wanted them to try out his new invention.

"I can always count on you and your friends to help me, Daphne!" he said.

Dash gave the gang a quick tour of his invention shop.

Shaggy and Scooby soon got into trouble.

"Ruh-roh!" cried Scooby.

"Like, how do we stop this crazy thing?" asked Shaggy.

On the way to the river, Shaggy looked for his lifejacket.

"Like, I think I might have left my lifejacket at home," said Shaggy.

"Not to worry," said Dash. "Here comes my assistant Mason. You can borrow his lifejacket."

Out on the river, the raft raced down the rapids.
"You didn't tell us what was so special about this
raft," said Fred.

"You'll see when we get to the waterfall,"
replied Dash.

"Zoinks!" cried Shaggy. "Like, did he just say
waterfall? We're out of here."

In a blink of an eye, they were at the waterfall.
"Here we go," said Dash. "Hold on tight!"
"A-a-a-h. . ." Shaggy screamed.
With a push of a button, wings popped out.
The raft gently floated down the side of the
waterfall.

But suddenly out of nowhere, a phantom eagle swooped in.

"Like, please tell us that's part of the invention!" said Shaggy.

"I don't know what that is," said Dash.

"Jeepers!" said Daphne. "It looks like it's headed right for us!"

The phantom eagle tried to bite Shaggy.
"Like, get away you feathery creep!" said Shaggy.

Back on shore, the gang examined what was left of Shaggy's lifejacket.

"Like, who makes lifejackets out of feathers and paper?" asked Shaggy.

"Hmm, that's odd. That's not any paper," said Velma. "That's a blueprint for Dash's new invention."

The next day the gang went to buy a new lifejacket.

"Look, there's Mason. That's weird. It looks like he's buying out the store," said Daphne.

Mason raced across the store to talk to the gang.

"Just looking at what's new for next season," he said.

Later that day, the gang helped Dash repair the raft.

"I just don't get who would want to ruin me," said Dash.

"Mason said my latest raft is all people are talking about."

"As luck would have it," said Daphne, "we've solved a mystery or two before."

As Dash and the gang finished the repair, the phantom eagle dove at them.

"Like, here comes that flying ghost again," said Shaggy.

"There's no time to lose," said Fred. "RUN!"

Dash and the gang ran for cover in his invention shop.
"We'll be safe in here," he said.

Inside the shop, Shaggy and Scooby had some fun.

"Jeepers!" said Daphne. "Watch it with the water balloons!"

Meanwhile, Fred spotted a hot air balloon raft.

"If that balloon flies," said Fred, "we can chase and catch that phantom."

Dash, Shaggy and Scooby were the bait.

"Like, this time I'm happy to be riding the rapids," said Shaggy.

"There's no way I want to be flying up there anywhere near that weirdo bird."

As the raft went over the falls, an eagle's screech could be heard across the canyons.

A moment later, the phantom eagle was swooping down on them.

"Zoinks!" cried Shaggy. "Duck!"

The phantom eagle was getting a little too close.

But the rest of the gang floated down in time to save the day.

"Ready, set, go!" said Fred. "Start throwing your water balloons."

With each hit, the phantom eagle lost more and more of its feathers.

It quickly fell into the river.

Dash, Shaggy, and Scooby were waiting on the shore to pull it in.

"The blueprint and feathers in your lifejacket gave you away, Mason," said Velma.

"How could you steal from me?" asked Dash.

"I knew I could be rich and famous if I stole your idea," said Mason.

"It would have worked, too, if it weren't for you meddling kids."

Dash gave the gang a big bear hug.

"Daphne," he said, "you and your friends really helped me out. How can I ever thank you?"

Shaggy led the gang toward Dash's invention shop.

"Like, I can think of one way," said Shaggy.

"Now this is my kind of invention!" said Shaggy, as they floated down the river. Scooby-Dooby-Doo!